This book belongs to:

. . . .

To my beautiful Lottie, for all the steps she's taken and all the steps to come. A.S.

This book is dedicated to Aslom for his work with children, and
to Jaime's admiration for him L.M.

OXFORD
UNIVERSITY PRESS

Great Clarendon Street, Oxford OX2 6DP
Oxford University Press is a department of the University of Oxford.
It furthers the University's objective of excellence in research, scholarship,
and education by publishing worldwide. Oxford is a registered trade mark of
Oxford University Press in the UK and in certain other countries

Text copyright © Amber Stewart 2010
Illustrations copyright © Layn Marlow 2010

The moral rights of the author and illustrator have been asserted
Database right Oxford University Press (maker)

First published as *Puddle's Big Step* in 2010
This edition first published in 2018

British Library Cataloguing in Publication Data
Data available

ISBN: 978-0-19-276852-0

10 9 8 7 6 5 4 3 2 1

Printed in China

Paper used in the production of this book is a natural,
recyclable product made from wood grown in sustainable forests.
The manufacturing process conforms to the environmental
regulations of the country of origin.

My First Milestones

My First Day

Amber Stewart • Layn Marlow

OXFORD
UNIVERSITY PRESS

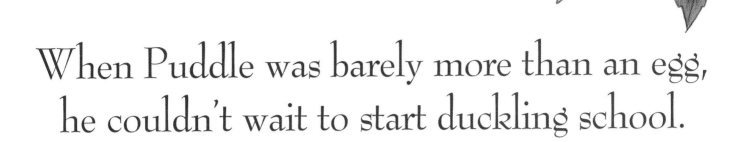

When Puddle was barely more than an egg,
he couldn't wait to start duckling school.

Every day, Puddle and his two friends, Pip and Fern, would watch the bigger ducklings waddling to and from Willow Brook Duckling School.

They looked so grown-up —
each with their own school bag . . .

and Puddle wished
to be just like them.

Then, one day, while Puddle was helping
Mummy to make his favourite biscuits,
Mummy gave him a big hug and said,
'Puddle, now *you* are big enough
to start duckling school.'

Puddle's feathers fluffed out with pride.

'Will I have my very own
school bag, Mummy?'
he asked.

'Yes you will,'
Mummy smiled.
'Your own special bag.'

But tucked up in their nest that night,
Puddle imagined his first day at school and
his little heart went pitter-patter, pitter-patter.

As he edged just that bit closer to Mummy's warm,
soft feathers, Puddle knew that he'd been wrong.
He *could* wait to go to duckling school . . .

he could wait until he was
a very old duck indeed.

'Every new little duckling at Willow Brook
will feel wobbly today,' Mummy said kindly,
slipping Puddle's bag over his wing.

'Your first day at school
is a very big step.'

But Puddle wasn't sure he could take even

one

very

small

step.

His feet
felt stuck to
the ground.

'You'll have fun,' smiled Mummy,
as she shooed him gently along the
stepping-stones into school.
'You're my brave little duck.'

As Puddle put down his school bag, he spotted
something . . . something very familiar.

It was one of Mummy's smallest, softest feathers.
She had tucked it inside to show she was never far away.

Then Puddle felt brave enough
to take his next big step . . .

and found a place to sit on the water-lily mat.
'I like your feather,' whispered the little duck beside him.

The morning went by in a flurry of . . .

matching
ladybirds . . .

counting
caterpillars . . .

and lily-pad leaping . . .

until their teacher clapped
her wings and asked them
all to settle down for lunch.

Puddle and Mummy had lunch together every day.
Suddenly, she did seem very far away.

But when Puddle took his lunch box
from his special bag, he found Mummy had
packed all his favourite nibbles . . .

and four best home-made biscuits —
one for him, one for Pip, one for Fern,
and one for a new friend, too.

After lunch, it was nap-time
under the willow tree.

Puddle peeped in his bag,
hoping that Mummy had
remembered his Cuddly . . .

and she had.

Later, all the ducklings made presents
for their mummies and daddies.

Some did
feet painting,

some made
daisy chains,

and some did
twig decorating.

At going-home time, Puddle tucked
his twig carefully into his bag, and ran
happily along the stepping-stones
for a warm, soft hug with Mummy.

Snuggled up in their nest that night,
Puddle thought about his first day at school
and his little heart went pitter-patter,
pitter-patter with excitement . . .

he couldn't wait to see
what he would do tomorrow
at duckling school.

My First Milestones
Ten Top Tips

If your toddler is starting pre-school or nursery,
like Puddle in this story, here are some hints and tips.

1 Prepare your toddler by talking about what they can expect at nursery.

2 Read picture books together about starting school (like this one!).

3 Share your own happy memories of your first days at school with your toddler.

4 Walk or drive past the school so that it becomes familiar.

5 Attend settling-in sessions together if they are offered.

6 Remember that it will be easier for your toddler at school if you help them with practical 'self-care' skills before they start.

7 Help your toddler to recognize their own name and put name labels on any items of uniform, lunchboxes, water bottles etc.

8 Create opportunities for your toddler to spend time with other children. This will help them get accustomed to sharing and taking turns.

9 Make sure your toddler can sit quietly and listen to instructions.

10 Practise your morning routine a few times before the big day arrives!